THE BROOCH

A SHORT STORY

GEETANJALI MUKHERJEE

CONTENTS

The Brooch: A Short Story

Geetanjali Mukherjee

© 2017 Geetanjali Mukherjee

Cover and book design: Geetanjali Mukherjee

ALSO BY GEETANJALI MUKHERJEE

Seamus Heaney: Select Poems

From Auden to Yeats: Critical Analysis of 30 Selected Poems

Illusions: A Collection of Poems

Creating Consensus: The Journey Towards Banning Cluster Munitions

Will The Real Albert Speer Please Stand Up? The Many Faces of Hitler's Architect

Goldilocks Lives in Leamington: and Other Tales of University Life in England

Negotiate, Persuade and Create Great Deals (co-authored with Michael Benoliel and Jose Yong)

The Smarter Student Series

Anyone Can Get An A+: How To Beat Procrastination, Reduce Stress and Improve Your Grades

Anyone Can Get An A+ Companion Workbook: How To Beat Procrastination, Reduce Stress and Improve Your Grades

Acing Standardized Tests: How To Study Smart, Reduce Stress and Improve Your Test Score

The Complete Writer Series

The Beginner Writer: How To Write - and Finish - Your First Book

The Beginner Writer Workbook: How To Write - and Finish - Your First Book

The Working Writer: Staying Creative Through The Seasons of Life

PRAISE FOR THE BROOCH

"The Brooch is an awesome short story, a quick yet powerful read. It reminded me what is important in life...We can forget what really matters. Michael Lim has a big secret that forces him and his wife, Grace, to each face where their priorities lie in this fable, and the resolution to the story is memorable. Simple but bold, I really enjoyed this one."
  - Dr. Aarti Patel, author

"The Brooch is an enchanting short story that gently reminds us of several life lessons: contentment with oneself and what one has, humility, and the true meaning of love... *The Brooch* is a simple, sweet, and flawlessly executed short story that invites the reader to reflect on themselves and their lives. It is a nice, feel-good story that will lift your spirits."
  - On My Kindle, book reviewer

"This is an enchanting story — seemingly quite simple, it carries ponderable meanings...This short but engaging tale clearly shows [Geetanjali's] talent as a true storyteller."
  - Alexander Zoltai, author

To my parents, who believed in my dream even when I didn't.

THE BROOCH

TODAY IS *the day I will definitely tell her*, Mr. Lim said to himself as he entered the elevator. Pressing the button for the 4th floor, he repeated the thought. *Yes, definitely today. This can't go on any longer.* He pulled the straps on his briefcase nervously, wondering how exactly he was going to broach this difficult subject with his wife.

Mr. Michael Lim was 58 years old, and today he felt every day of it. He shuffled his feet towards the door, feeling heavier with each step. He exited the elevator and rang the doorbell to flat #04-06. The maid answered, and took his briefcase without a word. "Is Mrs. Lim at home?" he enquired, while taking his shoes off at the door.

"She just got back, Sir."

Good, he may as well get it over with before he lost his nerve. It had been weeks, and he was sick of keeping it a secret. Just as he was thinking this, Mrs. Lim came bustling out of their bedroom. Mrs. Grace Lim was the polar opposite of her husband in every respect. Where he was tall and thin, with a slight bald patch in the middle of his head, she was squat and plump, with a well-coiffed hairdo and immaculately put-together outfits. Even when just popping down to the local shop to buy provisions, Mrs. Lim would ensure that she looked her best. After all, you never knew who you might run into.

"Oh good, you're back dear. How was the office? Same as usual? You will never guess the news I have to tell you. Actually I'm surprised you don't know already, after all Jeffrey must have brought it to the office."

Once his dear wife was on a roll, it was almost impossible to stop her. Partly grateful for the distraction, partly irritated by her self-interested prattle, Mr. Lim impatiently said: "What are you talking about?"

"Oh Jeffrey's new car of course!" Mrs. Lim responded as if it were patently obvious. "Dionne and I went out for lunch, and she couldn't stop talking about it. Jeffrey bought it only last week. Can you guess what it is? Only a sleek new black Porsch-a. Is that how you pronounce it? Or Porsche – with an e?"

A new car? But he said that business was down. Had he lied or was he being modest? It wasn't like Jeffrey to be modest. Mr. Lim realized the room had gone quiet, and his wife was looking at him expectantly. He had obviously tuned her out. "Sorry, what was that dear? I am quite hungry actually, is dinner ready?" He was hoping to distract her long enough for her to have found something else to talk about.

"I asked you if you have seen it? Jeffrey's new car? It must be very luxurious. Dionne said the seats are pure leather. It's got all the latest technology. And it runs very powerfully, according to Dionne."

Since when did his sister-in-law become such an expert on expensive cars? "No I haven't seen it. So what about dinner then?"

He hoped he would get a respite from this conversation at dinner. Maybe he could bring up the news he had been dreading telling her all day. He had been rehearsing this moment for weeks, but he still hadn't quite figured out how to broach the topic. Courage in confrontations was never Mr. Lim's strong suit, he preferred to take the easy way out. Presumably that was the same trait that had landed him in this situation, but he couldn't think of that at present. Worried about his wife's reaction, he found that he could barely touch the food she spooned on to his plate.

"What's the matter?", his wife demanded. "Isn't the *mee siam* cooked the way you like it? I told the girl to make it carefully, but I think her mind is never on the job. She is constantly texting someone. How many friends can she have here? She has only been here a few months."

"Anyway, Dionne was saying that already Jeffrey is getting so much more respect from his clients. He obviously looks successful, driving such an expensive car. I love my sister, but sometimes she can be such a show-off." Mrs. Lim tucked into the food on her plate with gusto.

She wasn't the only one, thought Mr. Lim. He knew where his wife was going with this. Any moment now, she would be saying that they too should get a new car.

"You know, dear, I think sometimes Dionne forgets I am her elder sister. I am three years older, and I deserve more respect from her. She was almost implying that her husband is more successful and that she did better in her choice of spouse than me. Can you imagine? As if. You are just a successful as Jeffrey. You work so hard, stay such long hours at the office. How dare she imply that we are not equally well off?"

Mrs. Lim gathered the plates from the table and took them to the kitchen. He could hear her putting together the makings for their ritual after-dinner cup of tea. She had obviously gotten herself into a state, judging by the bangs and crashes accompanying her actions. Mr. Lim didn't like to get in her way when she got all worked up like this. In so many ways, his wife was the polar opposite of her name. He loved her, but didn't want to get on her bad side.

Grace Lim brought the tray with the tea cups and kettle to the coffee table in the living room, a ritual she always liked to do herself, and one of the few things she never delegated to her maid. "Dear, I was thinking. Why don't we get a new car too? The one we have is so old the white is beginning to look grey. Besides, it is not the kind of car a successful real estate broker ought to be driving. After all, you have your reputation to think of. Why don't we look at some cars this weekend? Maybe we can get something even nicer than Jeffrey's. Won't that give them something to talk about?"

Mr. Lim mumbled something that he hoped sounded like an assent. He had no intention of looking at cars that weekend, or any time soon. But it was obvious: pompous Jeffrey and his showboating wife had ruined any chance for Michael to have that conversation with his wife. And he wasn't exactly sure that it wasn't a good thing.

MICHAEL PUT his hand out to lift up the coffee cup, when he realized that it was empty. Time for a refill. He put his newspaper down and looked at the large old-fashioned clock that hung on the wall opposite him. He was sitting in his favourite booth at his favourite neighbourhood coffee shop. The shop was part of a local chain that had opened nearly five decades ago; it was practically a national institution. And the owner's son was a childhood friend, who had arranged with staff for Mr. Lim to spend as much time as he liked in the shop, with unlimited coffee refills. Sometimes, they even threw in a slice of peanut butter toast. The toast was especially good, thick slices of whole wheat bread covered with a generous slathering of peanut butter.

Michael was grateful for the generosity of his childhood friend, especially as it meant that he could stay and read his paper for as long as he liked, whiling away the hours he would otherwise have been at work. It had only been a few weeks, but it felt like a lifetime ago. Every morning he got up, dressed the same way that he had for the past 30 years, picked up his briefcase and left home. The only difference was that instead of going to his office at the insurance firm where he worked, or rather used to work, he came to the coffee shop.

"We no longer have a space for you here", his brother-in-law had told him. "Business is down and things are quite bad at the moment. You haven't been bringing in any new clients for a while and we need to cut costs". And yet business couldn't be that bad if Jeffrey could buy a new Porsche.

Being kicked out of the firm where he had been a partner for 10 years was beyond humiliating. Mr. Lim had been so ashamed he couldn't tell anyone, even his wife, especially his wife. What she must think of him if she knew – hiding out at a coffee shop, unable to admit the truth. The only concession Jeffrey had made, was agreeing to keep Michael's leaving the firm a secret from his wife Dionne, Grace's sister. If Dionne knew, then Grace would know also, in a matter of minutes. Michael was grateful for the chance to tell his wife in his own time, although if he didn't do it soon, she might find out some other way. Jeffrey might tell Dionne, or someone else from the office might. *I have to do it tonight,* he told himself. *No more putting this off.* And he got up to get more coffee and a slice of toast. He was beginning to feel hungry – it was past his usual lunch time.

Just as he got up to ask the server behind the counter for a refill, he noticed a commotion near the front of the shop. Someone was yelling and he heard the sound of crashing coffee cups. *Whatever could have happened?*

Mr. Lim rushed up to the counter, where the server, who wasn't exactly conversant in English, was screaming in barely coherent Mandarin with large amounts of dialect thrown in. Apparently he had accidentally poured boiling hot water all over himself. The cashier, the only other employee in the shop, came rushing over to calm the server and take him to get help.

She looked at Mr. Lim with a note of panic in her voice, "I need to take Huizhong to the clinic. There is one just down the road. But I can't leave the shop like this, what do I do?"

She no doubt looked for guidance to Michael because she knew he was a friend of the owner. Just then a group of new customers walked in, the afternoon rush was just beginning. Closing up the shop clearly wasn't an option. Michael surprised himself and the cashier by saying, "Don't worry, I will take over serving till you can get back."

The grateful cashier didn't wait for him to change his mind, and rushed the still moaning Huizhong off to the clinic. Michael looked at the line of customers impatiently staring at him, and went behind the counter to pick up an apron. It dawned on him what exactly he had gotten himself into, and he started to doubt whether he could handle running a coffee shop by himself, with absolutely no experience. Why did he offer to help? *Because Teck Hoo is my friend. How could I not?*

After fumbling around a bit and making a few minor errors, he started to get the hang of it. Thankfully, most customers only asked for coffee and tea and cakes from the display shelves. Before he knew it, he found that he had gotten into a groove, and enjoyed the simple and rewarding work. He smiled at the customers, quickly counted up the change and managed to even make extra sales by offering add-on items to customers. His years of sales experience and dealing with clients held him in good stead. When the cashier returned to relieve him, he almost felt disappointed that he was no longer needed.

She informed him that she had taken the server to the hospital to be extra careful, and he was being well looked after. She thanked Mr. Lim profusely for helping out, almost sheepishly, knowing that it was highly unusual to rope in customers to help out. Michael was surprised to realize how much he had enjoyed his brief stint as a server cum cashier.

Michael looked at his watch and sighed. It was still early and his wife would probably wonder why he was home. It was the perfect opportunity to come clean with her, to tell her everything that had been going on. But instead he found himself coming up with excuses. It was getting easier and easier to lie to her. *When did I become this man? Why can I not tell my own wife the truth?* He told himself it was because his wife was difficult, she was too busy trying to keep up with the neighbours. She pressured him too much. But in his heart he knew that shifting the blame to Grace wasn't fair, that he had to own up to his problems and face their consequences.

On reaching home, Mr. Lim found that his wife wasn't there. He had forgotten that she had her weekly singing lesson with some of her neighbours from the building. *At least I can rest easy today. I can always tell her tomorrow.* With that, Mr. Lim put his feet up and picked up the remote to see what was good on TV.

~

THE NEXT MORNING, Michael was thinking about not leaving for the café. After the experience of the previous day, it would be weird to go back to simply sitting and reading the paper like nothing happened. He didn't realize how much he had missed working. But it wasn't just that. It was that he missed the feeling of being needed, of being useful. He hadn't had that feeling in such a long time, even before the trouble started at the firm.

At home he wasn't exactly seen as someone special. His children had grown up and left home. They didn't need him. They didn't even have time to call or come home anymore. Each week it was a different excuse. At the office he had ceased to be useful for a while. As he had grown older he had started to lose enthusiasm for this kind of life – the hard selling. The in-fighting. The posturing. Even before he was asked to leave, he had mentally checked out. He supposed he shouldn't be surprised that Jeffrey had asked him to leave. It was just a matter of time – he hadn't been getting as many sales as before. And as a partner, not only his bonus but his reputation depended on his results. It didn't help that the economy was down. He tried explaining all this to Jeffrey. Not that he should have needed any explanations. Jeffrey was as savvy as they came. He might be both his boss and his brother-in-law, but he had no illusions about his partner. Former partner he should say.

Just then his phone rang. It wasn't a number he recognized but he picked up anyway. A habit he had ingrained over years as a broker – you never knew when a client was calling.

"Hello, is that Michael Lim?", a familiar voice rang through the phone. A voice he couldn't immediately place. "Yes, this is he. Who is this?"

"Michael, this is Teck Hoo, from *Toast Shop*." Ah, now he had placed the booming voice. His childhood friend, owner of the coffee shop, had what people called a voice for radio. Ironically he didn't have a face for radio, being extremely good-looking and charming. Probably the reason he was now the owner of a multi-million-dollar empire.

"It's nice to hear from you, how have you been Teck Hoo? It has been too long. How is your employee? Was he too badly hurt?"

"That's why I am calling actually. We are short-handed because Huizhong is still in hospital. He isn't the smartest chap, but he is loyal to me. Have to make sure he recovers properly."

"Yes, yes, I know you have always done well by your people. So what is the reason for this call?" Michael was curious what prompted Teck Hoo to call him; despite spending almost every day at his coffee shop, Michael seldom saw his old friend anymore. He was busy running his empire, expanding coffee shops across the country. He was famously hands-on, and liked to see to every detail of each shop himself. He was extremely fussy about the kind of people he hired as well.

"So I heard about how you helped out yesterday at the shop after they rushed Huizhong to the hospital. Thanks for that by the way, I really appreciate it. I heard that you did really well – almost as if you have been doing this for years." Teck Hoo chuckled, and then rushed ahead before Michael could respond. "So I know this is unorthodox, but if you happen to have some time, could you help out again today? Just until I find a more permanent replacement for Huizhong?"

Mr. Lim hesitated for just a fraction of a second. Is this what he was really doing now? He had really enjoyed the chance to help out the other day, but what if someone saw him? What would his neighbours think? *It's only for a few days*, he thought to himself. What harm could it do? Besides he owed his friend, for a few hundred cups of coffee at the very least.

"Sure, I would be happy to help out. When do you need me to come in?"

Mrs. Grace Lim was getting ready to keep her standing appointment at the beauty salon when her mobile rang. It was her sister, Dionne.

"Oh hi, Dionne. How come you're calling at this time? Aren't you supposed to be at the hospital?"

Dionne Tan was 3 years younger than her sister Grace, and different in almost every way. She wasn't blessed with Grace's good looks, so she pretended that outer beauty did not matter to her, and focused on her inner beauty instead. Dionne's vanity limited itself to her character – she liked to think that she was a good person who did good things. She volunteered at the children's wing of the hospital a couple of times a week, reading them stories or bringing new toys to the children recuperating from whatever unfortunate illnesses they were suffering from. Her other source of vanity was her husband Jeffrey – she liked to push him out in the world; like a mother bird encouraging her baby to fly, she encouraged him to achieve greater heights.

"Oh actually, I am on my way to the hospital now. I stopped by to pick up some little cakes for the children. You know how I like to do little thoughtful things like that. It really makes their day, I know it does, when I visit those children. Poor things I feel, stuck in there, feeling so alone and miserable. I feel it is my duty to do all I can for them," Dionne said.

There she goes again, thought Grace. *Of course no one could ever measure up against Saint Dionne.* "I would have thought their parents would be visiting them regularly. They could hardly be alone," observed Grace dryly.

"Yes, well, I didn't say no one visits them." Grace could hear her sister bristling through the phone. She didn't like anyone to contradict her. "Anyway, the reason I called is to say that the funniest thing happened at the coffee shop." Dionne's voice had taken on a strangely strangled quality. Like she had a surprise, and not a good one.

Grace stiffened. She had no idea what Dionne was going to say, but something told her it wasn't good. *Probably just gossip about a mutual friend,* she told herself. Dionne wasn't malicious, but she could be a little morally high-handed.

"So I went in to get my order of cakes, and who did I see serving at the counter of *Toast Shop*," Dionne went barrelling on. "Your husband, of all people. I was so shocked that before he could notice me, I turned around and left the shop. I didn't want him to be embarrassed, especially in front of other people." Dionne sounded triumphant.

While talking to her sister Grace had been walking around the room, absent-mindedly straightening things, picking up things out of place and putting them right. She had been about to close the top drawer of her dresser, when she heard the words "your husband...serving coffee".

Followed by a crash. She had closed the drawer on her finger. She was so distracted, she didn't even notice the pain, despite the purplish tinge that immediately formed around its side.

"What was that noise?", demanded Dionne.

"Oh nothing, must be the helper. She is really clumsy, always dropping something. I better go see what she did. I will talk to you later!" Grace couldn't get off the phone fast enough.

She sat down on the chair beside the bed with a heavy sigh. Her husband, working in a coffee shop? Must be some kind of mistake. Surely he wouldn't do something like that. He had a good job, he was successful. He and Jeffrey were partners. And besides, wouldn't Dionne know if he had stopped working at her husband's firm? Maybe this was her sister's idea of a joke. *Not funny*, she thought to herself.

Her hair appointment forgotten, Grace rushed out to see for herself what Dionne was talking about. All the way there she kept telling herself that it was a mistake, some elaborate practical joke, something she could laugh about later, though she wasn't sure she could see any humour in this situation. Grace wasn't exactly known for her sense of humour, or her ability to display grace under pressure. She never simply accepted a situation, she usually got what she wanted, one way or another. And what she wanted was to know why her husband was intent on humiliating her and bringing shame to the family.

MICHAEL LIM WAS WORKING at the coffee shop. Wearing an apron, he felt as if he had been doing this for years, not hours. Taking orders, serving coffee and cake, this was the most fun he had had in some time. At the same time, he was aware that he would not be able to do this for long. The server would get better, and he would come back to claim his job. More importantly, he could not do this for long. He shuddered at the thought of telling his wife. "Honey, I work at *Toast Shop* now." He could only imagine how that conversation would go. Not well, he was sure.

At that moment he looked up and almost dropped the cup he was holding with a shock. Had he conjured up Grace's scowling face in his imagination? Strange, because she looked pretty real.

"What are you doing, Michael?" Uh oh, she never called him Michael. Unless she was really mad.

"I can explain dear." Mr. Lim stammered, while acutely aware of the line forming behind his wife, and the surprised expressions on the faces of the other patrons.

"Really, I highly doubt that. I want you to come out from behind that counter right now. We can talk about this at home."

Maybe bravado would work. "There is nothing to talk about. I am helping out Teck Hoo. One of his workers had an accident, and he asked me to fill in as a favour." His voice wavered slightly, but he pressed on. "I can't leave now. I need to be here. I will see you later at home."

He was not surprised to see that the expression on his wife's face was unchanged, but he could also tell that she was willing to postpone the argument. Obviously she cared more about creating a scene and embarrassing herself than dressing him down. *Small mercy,* he thought. As he busied himself serving the next customer in line, he glanced over to where his wife was standing a few moments before. She had gone, and what she had left unsaid hung in the air between them.

GRACE SAT in her favourite chair in front of the TV, staring into space, her cup of tea forgotten on the side table next to her. She was wrestling with herself – on one hand, her mother had taught her that her job as a wife was to always be at her husband's side. And that is precisely what she had done her whole life. Hadn't she been the model wife, hosting parties for important clients and always trying to look and be the perfect corporate wife? Then what had gone wrong? Wasn't it now her husband's turn to ensure that he was the perfect corporate husband? How could he humiliate her like this?

Mrs. Lim made a decision. Enough of sitting here feeling sorry for herself. She would pack her things and move to her sister's house, at least for a few days. She needed time to think. Her sister Dionne might be shallow and full of herself, but at least she was family. She would never turn her back on her only sister.

She curtly asked her helper to bring her overnight bag, and started to rustle through her drawers throwing things in randomly. Despite her determination to maintain a calm façade, Mrs. Lim was feeling far from calm. Normally impeccably organized, her erratic packing was the only outward side of her inner turmoil. *I have to focus*, she told herself. *I can't turn up at my sister's place with mismatched things.* Knowing that she must maintain her image even at this time, she opened the drawer where she kept her jewellery, intending to pack just a few choice items.

Rummaging through her jewellery drawer, Mrs. Lim's hands closed around a small box wrapped with faded hand-made paper. She couldn't place this box – where had it come from? What did it contain? As soon as she opened it, she gasped involuntarily.

Nestled inside the faded edges of the box was a brooch; shaped in the form of a butterfly, it was well-worn, but colourful. As she lifted the brooch out of the box, Grace's hands shook. She had forgotten about this brooch – tucked away at the back of her jewellery drawer. This was the first gift Mr. Lim had given her, back when they were courting. He had a job that barely covered his expenses, and he lived very simply, saving as much of his income as he could. It was her birthday, and she hadn't really expected much. They had both grown up in humble circumstances, and while she dreamed of pretty things, the reality was that there was very little money for luxuries. She had been incredibly surprised and touched to receive this gift from Michael for her birthday.

She later found out that he had scoured many shops, looking for something beautiful but inexpensive to give her. When he gave her the brooch, wrapped with tissue paper inside the very same box she was now holding in her hand, he had said: "I know that this is not very expensive, but I hope that you will take it as a token of the life that we will make together, and of all the beautiful things that I will eventually buy for you. I hope that every time you look at it, you remember that it reflects my love for you."

Grace had been surprised more by that speech than by the gift itself. It was a beautiful brooch, even though she knew that it wasn't worth very much. What made it special to her was the sentiment behind it, which is why she kept it safely all these years. Every time she looked at it, and she used to look at it a lot in those first years of marriage, she would remember how lucky she was to have found a man who loved her so much.

Over the years, Michael had kept his promise. He had bought her many expensive pieces of jewellery and branded handbag and taken her on luxurious holidays. She had gotten used to beautiful things and expensive gifts. And over time, she had forgotten about that brooch and the simple promise it represented.

For Grace, the brooch had represented not only Michael's promise to her, but her own vow to love and cherish him. She remembered that promise now, and reflected no longer on how Michael had let her down, but on how *she* had failed *him*.

〜

MICHAEL STEPPED out of the lift, and his stomach growled involuntarily. The air was fragrant with the smell of his favourite food. One of the neighbours must be having guests, although it was strange that they hadn't been invited. Perhaps the neighbours too had gotten wind of his troubles and decided to distance themselves from him. He shook himself mentally, it wasn't like him to be brooding or self-pitying. But then, he knew what was awaiting him at home.

Ever since he had seen Grace at the coffee shop, he knew the game was up. No doubt his wife would be angry about him losing his job, but she would be angrier still that he had kept it from her. If only he had not hidden it from her, and told her before she could find out from someone else.

Hesitating for a fraction of a second, he rang the bell. As the door was opened by the helper, the smell of food was overpowering. "Is Mrs. Lim home?", he asked the helper.

"Yes, Ma'am is in the kitchen", came the response.

Intriguing. His wife almost never cooked anymore. Not

unless they had company. Perhaps his sister-in-law was over. Which probably wasn't a good sign. Maybe his wife felt she needed reinforcements.

Just then Grace emerged from the kitchen. "Oh, you're home dear. Why don't you freshen up and come to the table? Dinner is about ready."

As he took his place at the head of the table, Mr. Lim was surprised. His wife was smiling, not distracted or complaining, as she usually did when he came home. She had cooked, and nothing about her expression suggested that she was the same person who only hours earlier was furious with him at the coffee shop. What had changed? Was this an unusually creative and cruel way for her to announce that she was leaving him?

As he was thinking, Grace sat down next to him and filled first his plate, then hers. "I made your favourite dishes today. I thought you would appreciate it, why aren't you eating?"

"I do appreciate it. I can't believe you went to all this trouble." He hesitated, then gathering his courage, went on. "I don't know what you must think about the coffee shop earlier. I should have told you everything a long time ago. I am so sorry."

It was only then that he noticed the brooch on her dress. *It couldn't be the same one, could it? But it had been so long.*

Grace noticed her husband staring at the brooch, and said: "Yes, I know what you're thinking, it's the same one. I found it today while clearing out some stuff. Do you remember when you gave it to me?"

"Yes, I remember quite clearly. I can't believe you kept it all this time". Michael smiled nostalgically.

"Of course, I kept it," said Mrs. Lim with a smile. "It

was the first gift you ever gave me. I loved it. And I love you. No matter what."

He took that last statement as a sign. "Then I need to tell you something." And he finally told her everything. About losing the job, and how he had been pretending to go to work every day while hiding out at the coffee shop. About the way Jeffrey had treated him, and that he had felt so humiliated and defeated, he couldn't say or do anything. How he was so afraid to tell her, because he had let her down.

"You have never let me down. It is me who has failed to live up to my promise as a wife. When you gave me this brooch, you were not the only one who made a promise. I too vowed that I would love you, all my life. That I would support you and do my best to make you happy. I forgot that. I got caught up keeping up with my friends and focusing so much on material things. I am sorry that you couldn't come to me with your problems, that you had to bear the burden on your own." Her eyes filled with tears, and he reached out and put his hand on hers.

This was the most affectionate and honest conversation they had had in months, maybe in years. Maybe losing his job was a good thing for Michael – he no longer needed to pretend that he was successful or happy just to keep appearances going. He was happier now, at this moment, than he had been for months. Maybe things would turn around. As soon as he got himself another job.

"Tomorrow I will start looking for other sales jobs. I was having trouble earlier, but I am sure it is a matter of time. Don't worry dear, I will find something to support us."

"I'm not worried," said Mrs. Lim. "You have always supported us before and I know you will in the future too.

But what about the job at the coffee shop? Do you not still have that?"

"But I thought you would not want me to work there? I mean it's not very prestigious, and what will everyone think?"

"I don't care about prestige anymore. It was all so silly. If the job makes you happy, then I am happy. Would you like to work at the coffee shop? Or would you like to go back to sales?" Mrs. Lim busied herself clearing the dishes from the table.

"Actually I love working at the coffee shop, more than I thought I would. To be honest, I had begun to hate my sales job, and losing it was a relief in some ways. I didn't realize till I started at the coffee shop how much I had dreaded going to work every day. And in fact, today Teck Hoo offered me a managerial role. I don't know all the details, but I think I will enjoy working with my old friend."

"Then it's settled. You will do what makes you happy and we will figure the rest out. When you gave me this brooch we promised to make each other happy, no matter what happened. I want you to be happy, that will make me happy too. We have each other, everything else will work itself out." Mrs. Lim busied herself preparing the cups for their post-dinner cup of tea.

As they settled down companionably on the sofa to enjoy their tea, Mr. Lim looked at his wife, and realized that despite losing his job, he was very lucky. He still had the love of his life, and that made him very rich indeed. Mrs. Lim sipped her tea, while fingering her brooch, and knew that her mother had been right all along.

ABOUT THE AUTHOR

Geetanjali Mukherjee grew up in India, spending her early years in Kolkata, and then attending high school in New Delhi. She went on to read law as an undergraduate at the University of Warwick, United Kingdom, where she joined as many clubs as possible while still giving the impression she understood the intricacies of trusts law. She went on to earn a Masters' in Public Administration from Cornell University, United States, while trying not to freeze along with the famed Ithaca lakes. She is also a member of Pi Alpha Alpha, the Global Honor Society for Public Affairs and Administration.

Geetanjali is the author of thirteen books, although sometimes it feels like she is writing the very first one. Her books have been translated into seven languages. Geetanjali currently lives in Singapore.

If you liked the story, I would really appreciate a short review (even one line) on the retailer page or on Goodreads. Your help is gratefully appreciated as reviews make a huge difference in helping readers choose their next read. Thank you!

facebook.com/geetumuk

instagram.com/geetumuk

threads.com/@geetumuk

Goldilocks Lives in Leamington:
And Other Tales of University Life in England

Born For The Stage

When I was in elementary school, in the first school production I was in, I played the vitally important role of a tree. In the next one, I was promoted; I played a sheep. A few years later, I actually had a role that required me to move around the stage and even included a tiny speaking (or rather shouting) role: I was a peasant during the French Revolution. My career of triumph on the stage in school probably led me to decide that I needed to find more avenues for my acting talent.

At the beginning of each term, the Student's Union held a bazaar to let all the societies and clubs advertise their wares, to let us know how awesome each of these clubs was and why we should join. The event was held in the dark, slightly claustrophobic basement, which itself had the feel of an underground club - one of those shady ones where you expect to encounter a drug deal taking place in the darkest corner.

When I walked in with my friends after class that day, I was hoping that the line we had been fed – "Find your future friends here! Find a like-minded community!" was actually true and we would stumble on a ready-made set of friends simply by joining the right club. My friend Soph and I wandered around the basement, slightly blinded by the combination of the weird underground lighting and the enthusiastic people jumping out of every booth, shoving flyers in our face or extolling the virtues of their own society. And all I could think was, *Well, this all sounds very nice, if only I wouldn't have to spend time with the actual members of the club.* Because if they were anything like the people I had just met, I knew I wouldn't be able to spend more than five minutes with these perky, cheerful, Energizer bunnies. I think Soph and I gave up after half an hour, and decided to simply look online at the list of societies and pick something.

The irony didn't occur to me then - of finding a virtual solution to the problem of how to find people to spend time with in person - and remember, this was pre-Facebook, where you could have hundreds of "friends" and have only ever interacted with most of them through a screen. We were still old-fashioned then, and had to shower and wear clothes in order to meet people.

So anyway, we went through the list of societies and chose the ones that seemed the most promising. I picked some very, shall we say, eclectic ones, hoping that something would click and I would find an instant tribe. One of my choices was oddly, an acting society named *Codpiece*. I don't think I ever figured out the origin of that name, but maybe that's because I didn't make it as far as the annual summer barbecue, or even till the Xmas social, when no doubt, all secrets would have been revealed.

As I mentioned, Codpiece was an acting club, but with a twist. The main activity was that the members conceived, rehearsed and performed a play over a weekend. Perhaps the reduced time commitment was why I signed up for this particular experience, without realizing that spending an entire weekend learning lines, cobbling together a costume and actually performing a play was probably far more intense than spreading it out over time.

At the first meeting of the club, we were randomly assigned partners to work with and I was put in a group with two other guys. They were both first years as well I think, but other than that, I don't remember anything else about them. Ironic, since the main purpose of this was to get to know more people, and make friends, but I think my group partners spontaneously realized they didn't want to be friends with me, and I may have independently come to the same conclusion. So, of course, now we were stuck together for an entire weekend.

To facilitate the process, each group was handed a script, and we were supposed to put together a play based off of that. In retrospect, I wonder why there were no guide-lines, no instructions issued, no "here's the basics of acting and putting together a play in 10 minutes" kind of speech. Anyway, with the unbridled enthusiasm of youth and inex-perience, we simply jumped in and assigned parts.

And this is where things really got interesting. In a huge step-up from "second tree from the left" and "peasant shouting slogans", I got the starring role. In yet another twist of fate, the play we were assigned dramatized a different but equally famous story from French history: that of Joan of Arc. As in, the famous French woman (girl, really), who people thought was batty, since she claimed to be able to talk to God, and sent to the stake, but was actually deeply patriotic and wanted to save France.

The "play" was really a couple of scenes from the story, and since we were only three people in a group, there wasn't much we could do in terms of huge productions. Since I was the only woman, I was assigned the role of Joan, and I bet the other guys weren't too thrilled that I got the starring part; probably one of the contributing factors to them then proceeding to give me the cold shoulder.

Given that we were meant to be putting the whole thing up over a weekend, and the first time we clapped eyes on the script was a Friday evening, the script luckily wasn't very long, and there weren't many lines to memorize. But then again, I was supposed to be Joan of Arc. I had the main part. So if *I* forgot my lines, it would be kind of obvious. And if I freaked, or stumbled, or stared into space, again, obvious. And to make matters worse, due to our collective lack of experience, it didn't occur to us to do a run-through. We didn't prep our lines into the wee hours of Sunday morning. In fact, I get the distinct impression that my co-actors couldn't wait to run out the door after the first rehearsal, where we basically talked about what we were planning to do, and then each went our separate ways. In hindsight, that might have been a telling detail. That my co-actors weren't that invested in the project. That none of us fought for extra rehearsal time. That we didn't suggest a dress rehearsal, or try to find some props.

I guess the guys in my group chose this particular activity just as haphazardly as I did. And the "finish a play in a weekend" part must have appealed to them as well, signalling that they could add an extra-curricular activity with minimum participation - a couple of hours each day.

Thankfully, as a first-year student the stakes were pretty low - this was hardly the West End or Broadway. It wouldn't even qualify as off-off-off-Broadway. This was more in the region of Joey's ill-fated rendering of Freud as a singing psychiatrist.

When I was in school and resentful at being fobbed off with the insignificant roles of flora and fauna and dim-witted villagers, I wished ardently that for once I could get a real speaking part, one where I could display the acting prowess that I was sure I had. After years of longing for my moment under the spotlight, I had probably never stopped to wonder whether I had any talent for the stage. Careful what you wish for I suppose, because here I was with the leading role and quite sure that a squeaking or barfing version of Joan of Arc wouldn't exactly pass muster.

Sunday morning came and with it the realization that I was going on stage to play a French icon. I called my dad in a panic - what was I thinking and why had I gotten myself into this? I couldn't act. What if I didn't remember my lines? What if I bombed? And the audience wanted to burn me at the metaphorical stake? Or worse - *walked out*? In a fit of mad euphoria, I had invited my entire dorm floor to attend. Some of them had even said they would come. Perhaps nothing else exciting was happening on a Sunday afternoon. Could I really make a right fool of myself in front of these people, most of whom didn't have that amazing an opinion of me at the best of times? Not to mention, that if I were thoroughly humiliated, I would still have to see them every day for the rest of the year!

I only managed to convey some of this to my dad, and he tried to reassure me. He said that I would do a great job, to which I replied, "How do you know that?" In fairness, he didn't, but what else was he supposed to say really? And quickly too, since this call was costing a fortune. This was way before smartphones and FaceTime, when you had to go to a dodgy shop in town and buy a calling card to call home. Quite improbably, my dad actually managed to say something that calmed me down and made me believe for a minute or so that I could do this. He reminded me that the essence of Joan (I might as well be on intimate terms with someone I was going to impersonate on stage) was that she really cared about her country and her people. She wanted to save them.

My dad reminded me that that was all I had to do - dig down deep within my own experiences, my own misguided but noble notions (not my dad's words) of saving the world as a lawyer. This was it - somehow I had stumbled onto a technique that enabled me to tap into that thing I read about somewhere - method acting. Where you try to put yourself into the character's shoes. And become them. In as much as I could become a 15-year old French soldier who thought she heard God talking to her. (Unfortunately, this was the extent of my knowledge of Joan of Arc, clearly, I hadn't been paying enough attention in history class.)

I also reminded myself that I wasn't entirely a novice at this acting thing. When I was in high school, I acted in a short educational film on non-violence, sharing screen space for just a moment with a well-known Indian movie actress and director. Mind you, I wasn't exactly going to win any acting awards, especially given that I had to deliver my lines in a language that I didn't have a great command of at the best of times. I also took an acting workshop for an entire summer, with the National School of Drama in India, where I managed over time to let go of a lot of my inhibitions (making funny faces and leaping around a room in absurd poses will do that to you), learnt a variety of acting techniques that I then promptly forgot, and collectively put on a play to which our respective families were invited. I even helped to direct parts of that play, which in retrospect may not have been the most enriching experience for those *being* directed.

At any rate, so far I probably had more experience with acting than most of the others who had joined the society. Strangely, however, I seemed to be the most nervous. Probably because I knew exactly how bad we really were going to be.

When the time came for our group to perform, I said a silent prayer, and murmured my first few lines to myself so I would have a head-start. As the curtain went up, (actually there was no curtain, just an announcer who inevitably mangled the pronunciation of my name) I stepped out onto the stage, just as foolhardy as Joan, with just as much belief in myself, she thinking she could free France, me believing that I could act, wearing a blue Kashmiri kaftan of my mums', hoping it would pass as the garb of a French villager from the 15th century.

Shock and denial have wiped out most of the memories of my actual performance. I know I delivered my lines, mostly in the correct order. I even overcame my stage fright once I got on stage, getting into the spirit of the narrative. I probably overacted, brandishing my prop sword with gusto. What I do remember most vividly is getting off the stage, and feeling equal parts sheepish that I undertook something so crazy, relieved that it was over, and proud that I had come through it without embarrassing myself too terribly. I also remember my dorm mates, who had unexpectedly come out in large numbers to see my thespian debut, and they tactfully refrained from commenting on just how mortifyingly bad our performance really was, and we all went out for a nice filling roast dinner afterwards.

While I was in college, this weekend was just a blip, something I did on a lark. I ended up quitting Codpiece even before I officially joined – we had a few weeks before we had to pony up and pay to be part of the club and all its activities – and my disastrously short-lived stage career was just a distant memory of something else I did that I could blame on youthful exuberance. But back in the real world, I envied the version of myself that had the courage to do something at which I was highly likely to make a fool of myself. In my first year of college, I didn't know any better. I didn't think that I could be humiliated or that I may not have the requisite talent to do something. I simply jumped in with both feet, and realised later what kind of swamp I was standing in. In later years, when I was tempted to walk away from something that could be fun but also had the potential to be embarrassing, I tried to remember what it felt like to take a risk that might not work out, that could end up with me metaphorically tripping and falling on my face. And I would remind myself of the time when I stood in a blue kaftan, waved about a prop sword, and tried to save France.

This is an excerpt from my book Goldilocks Lives in Leamington: My Quirky Adventures As An International Student in England, *a collection of humorous essays about my years as an international student in the UK.*